Parent's Introduction

Whether your child is a beginning reader, a reluctant reader, or an eager reader, this book offers a fun and easy way to encourage and help your child in reading.

Developed with reading education specialists, **We Both Read** books invite you and your child to take turns reading aloud. You read the left-hand pages of the book, and your child reads the right-hand pages—which have been written at one of six early reading levels. The result is a wonderful new reading experience and faster reading development!

You may find it helpful to read the entire book aloud yourself the first time, then invite your child to participate the second time. As you read, try to make the story come alive by reading with expression. This will help to model good fluency. It will also be helpful to stop at various points to discuss what you are reading. This will help increase your child's understanding of what is being read.

In some books, a few challenging words are introduced in the parent's text, distinguished with **bold** lettering. Pointing out and discussing these words can help to build your child's reading vocabulary. If your child is a beginning reader, it may be helpful to run a finger under the text as each of you reads. Please also notice that a "talking parent" ☺ icon precedes the parent's text, and a "talking child" ☺ icon precedes the child's text.

If your child struggles with a word, you can encourage "sounding it out," but keep in mind that not all words can be sounded out. Your child might pick up clues about a word from the picture, other words in the sentence, or any rhyming patterns. If your child struggles with a word for more than five seconds, it is usually best to simply say the word.

Most of all, remember to praise your child's efforts and keep the reading fun. After you have finished the book, ask a few questions and discuss what you have read together. Rereading this book multiple times may also be helpful for your child.

Try to keep the tips above in mind as you read together, but don't worry about doing everything right. Simply sharing the enjoyment of reading together will increase your child's reading skills and help to start your child off on a lifetime of reading enjoyment!

Little Chipper

A We Both Read Book
Level K–1

We Both Read® is a trademark of Treasure Bay, Inc.

Published by Treasure Bay, Inc.
P.O. Box 119
Novato, CA 94948 USA

Printed in Malaysia

Library of Congress Catalog Card Number: 2016940080

Hardcover ISBN: 978-1-60115-295-4
Paperback ISBN: 978-1-60115-296-1

Visit us online at:
www.webothread.com

PR-11-16

WE BOTH READ®

Little Chipper

By Sindy McKay

Illustrated by Sydney Hanson

TREASURE BAY

Hi there! I'm Chipper. I'm on my way to the park. My friends and I **love** the park.

Last night it rained, so there will be lots of mud.

I love mud!

Some of my friends are big. Some are **small**. Some are fast. Some are slow. Some are boys. Some are girls.

King is big.

I am **small.**

Today there is a new dog in the park. He has a bright green tennis ball.

"I'm Rex," he barks. "Want to play?"

 "Yes! Yes! Yes!"

Chasing a ball is one of our favorite things to do **here** in the park.

Rex flings the ball and shouts, "Go!"

8

Here we go!

My friend **King** gets to the ball first. He's the fastest dog in the park. He's also really nice.

King is the best!

Now it's King's turn to fling the ball. He gives me a head start. (He always gives me a head start because I am so small.)

Here we go!

Rex quickly catches up to me. I guess he doesn't see me though, because he trips right over me.

Spot runs past us and gets the ball. He is happy!

Rex is mad.

"This little dog got in my way," Rex growls.

I say I'm sorry, but he still looks mad.

Now it's Spot's turn to sling the ball.

Here we go!

Rex gets to the ball first, so I stop to smell a flower. I guess Rex doesn't see me stop because he trips over me again and drops the ball. I pick it up.

Whee! I am **happy**!

 Rex is not **happy**.

I give the ball
to Princess.

Princess gives it
to Posey.

Posey gives it
to Tim. Then we
all run together
to give the ball
to Spot.

Here we go!

Everyone is having a great time! Everyone except Rex, that is.

"I **feel** like that little dog is always in my way," he complains.

 I **feel** bad.

King smiles at me and says, "Come on! Let's just play!" He flings the ball.

I try my best not to get in Rex's way. Then I see something.

A cat is in the tree!

 "Hey, guys," I shout. "Fluffy is here!"

The other dogs stop chasing the ball and run over to greet her.

Fluffy is happy to see us!

Rex is not happy.
Rex is mad.

Rex tells everyone, "Chipper cannot play with us anymore. He is too small and too slow and he stops to talk to cats! Either he goes or I go. And I'll take my ball with me."

"Here I go."

I don't want the game to stop. Everyone is having fun. So I ask Rex to please stay. I won't play. I'll just sit and watch.

I don't really want to just watch.

I am sad.

My friends don't **seem** to know what to do.

Then King says, "If Chipper can't play, then neither will I." He smiles at me. "Let's go find some mud, Chipper!"

Rex watches us go.

Rex **seems** happy.

"**Thank** goodness that little dog is gone,"
he barks. "Now let's play ball!"

Rex flings the ball, but no one moves.

"Go," he **says**. "Run after it!"

"No **thank** you,"
says Tim.

Rex wonders why Tim and the other dogs won't play.

Princess explains, "We always play together. You want to leave Chipper out. That's not nice."

"We're going to play in the mud with Chipper," says Spot.

Rex is sad.

Rex sits alone for a while.

Then King goes and asks him if he'd like to play in the mud with us.

Rex looks hopeful. "You'll let me?"

King nods. "We let *everyone* play."

Rex is happy.

"I love mud!"

Rex jumps into a big puddle. Mud splashes everywhere!

Then he says, "I'm sorry, Chipper. I shouldn't have said you can't play. It wasn't nice."

That makes me happy.

"Come on, Rex," I say. "Let's play!"

"Here we go!"

If you liked *Little Chipper,* here are some other
We Both Read® books you are sure to enjoy!

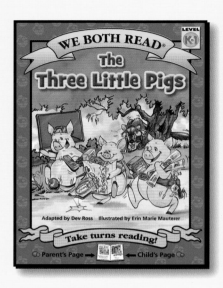